MY SPECIAL CHRISTMAS ADVENTURE

This book was especially written for Nicholas Dalbis with love from Mom and Dad

Written by Julia Wilson
&
Margaret Gibson
Illustrated by Ester Kasepuu

It was Christmas Eve!
The green Christmas Tree stood tall and wide, covered with sparkling tinsel. Bright ornaments gleamed from it and at the very top was a beautiful angel.
On the mantelpiece above the fireplace was a piece of cake and a glass of milk.

It was time for bed, but Nicholas Dalbis sat wondering when Santa Claus would visit him at 2 Scott Lane, Lagrangeville. He gazed at the beautiful tree he had decorated with Peter, Taylor and Peter.

Shining baubles, tiny animals, Father Christmase
golden bells and silver stars reflected the flames
from the fireplace. The whole room seemed magica

Nicholas looked up at the Christmas angel on the tree and asked,

'My Christmas angel, how does Santa bring presents to children in so many places all over the world?'

Fluttering her fine golden wings, the angel said,
'Dear child, there are many different ways Santa delivers presents. Would you like to help him this year? He is always needing helpers.'
And as she spoke, thousands of glittering stars shot from her fingertips and filled the room.

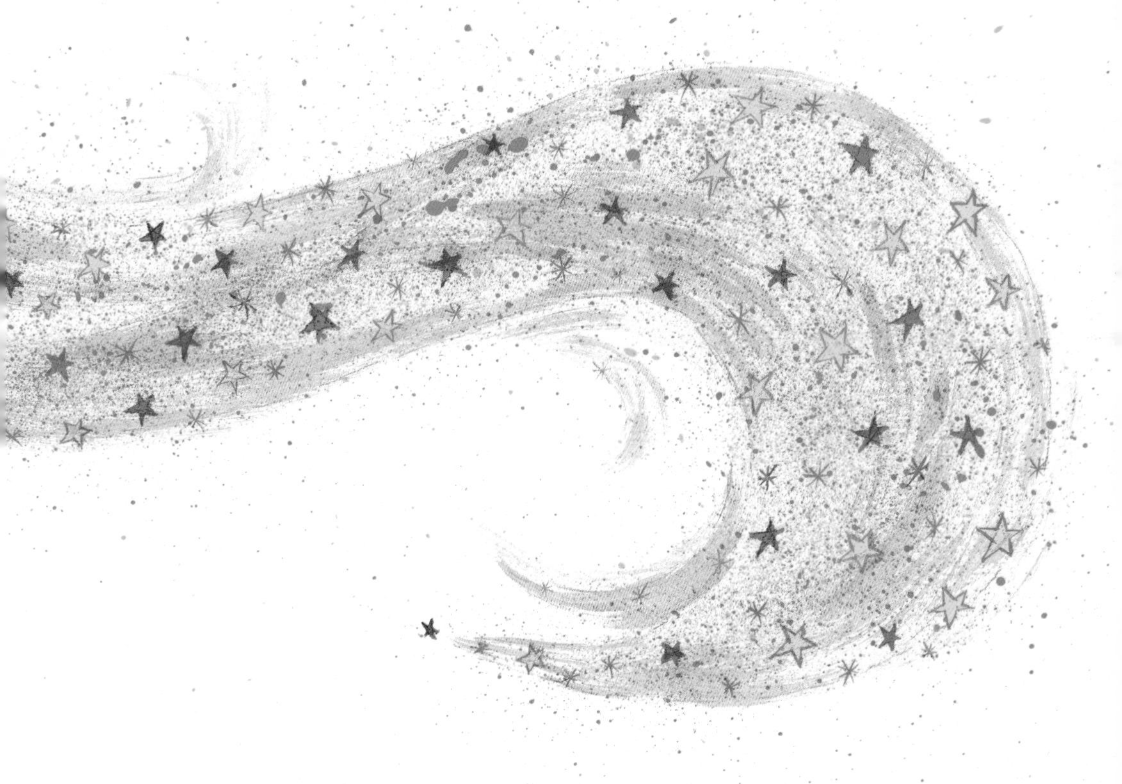

Nicholas was so surprised that he could not speak, so he nodded his head.
He felt himself being gently lifted among the glittering stars and seconds later he was standing in the workshop of Santa Claus!

Hundreds of tiny elves were busily wrapping Christmas presents. There were little presents, big presents, long, round and oddly shaped presents. At one end of the workshop a huge sleigh was being filled with more presents.

A door opened and in came Santa Claus himself!
'Hello, Nicholas,' he smiled. 'I am so pleased to see you.'

'How do you know my name?' asked Nicholas.

'I know all about you,' said Santa. 'I even know that you were born on the twenty-third of March.'

'You are my special helper this year and I want you to help me deliver all these presents to children around the world,' said Santa, climbing into his sleigh.
The elves pushed the sleigh out onto the crisp white snow and harnessed the waiting reindeer. Hovering nearby was the Christmas angel.

Nicholas ran out through the doorway and called,

'Wait Santa! Is there really room for me?'

Santa nodded and helped him into the sleigh.

'Could Peter, Taylor and Peter come with me?' he asked.

'Not tonight, Nicholas,' replied Santa. 'This is your special adventure.'

The reindeer were stamping their hoofs
and snorting with impatience. Santa grasped
their reins and called:

'Now, Dasher! Now, Dancer!
Now, Prancer and Vixen!
On, Comet! On, Cupid!
On, Donner and Blitzen!'

Their antlers glistening with snowflakes,
the eight reindeer ran swiftly across the snow.
Faster and faster they ran, until very smoothly
and gently they began climbing into the
starry sky.
As the huge sleigh lifted from the snow,
Nicholas felt as though he was flying to the
moon.

'Did you know that the United Kingdom is quite close to my workshop?' cried Santa, who was now wearing very curly whiskers. 'Look down there!' Far beneath them was the tall Christmas Tree in Trafalgar Square, London. 'Each Christmas,' Santa said, 'the people of Norway send a tree as a gift to the people of England.'

As they flew towards the roofs and chimneys, Nicholas could see the sparkling lights on the tree.

'Here children also call you Father Christmas,' said Nicholas. 'And you will find stockings to fill.' Santa disappeared into each house and filled the children's stockings.

'Not a moment to lose!' he called, jumping into the sleigh as it took off again.

They flew across Holland without stopping.

'I delivered their presents on Sinterklaas Eve,' explained Santa. 'Every sixth of December I visit on my white horse with my helper, Peter. All the people welcome me and call me Sinte Klaas or Saint Nicholas.'

All Europe twinkled with candles lit to welcome friends and strangers. The reindeer and sleigh gently landed in Sweden.

'Now I will be very busy,' sighed Santa. 'Here I am the Tomten and I go from house to house.' Knock, knock!

'It's the Tomten. Are there any kind and good children here?'

As each door opened he handed presents to the children.

They flew on. As they neared Germany the Christmas angel whispered to Nicholas,

'Now it's my turn to help Santa.'

Leaving a trail of sparkling stars, she flew down, down, down...

'Where is she going?' Nicholas asked Santa.

Santa smiled and said, 'She is the Christkindl
She flies through the windows and rings
a silver bell warning the children to go to bed.
While they sleep she fills their empty soup
bowls with fruits and sweets for them to find
on Christmas morning.'

What a busy night!
Soon they were flying high over Santa's home at the North Pole to deliver presents to the children of the United States. The only sounds that Nicholas could hear were the swoosh of the sleigh and the jingle of the tiny bells that hung from the reindeer harness.

The reindeer pulled the sleigh down towards the bright lights.

'You know that each Santa Claus you see at department stores and on street corners is my special helper, too,' said Santa. 'I cannot get to every place in the world at the same time.'

Santa was once again wearing his red hat with a pom-pom. Nicholas handed him each present as he moved swiftly through doors and windows and scrambled down chimneys, taking presents to the sleeping children of the United States.

The reindeer turned the sleigh to the south-west, across the wide Pacific Ocean.

'I could do with some cake and a glass of milk,' said Santa. 'This work is making me quite hungry and thirsty.'

Nicholas smiled to himself.
High in the sky again Santa pointed to the sparkling stars.

'That's the Southern Cross,' he cried. 'I use those stars to guide me to the children of New Zealand and Australia.'

They landed in New Zealand. Santa smiled and said, 'New Zealand is also called...'

'The Land of the Long White Cloud!' said his special helper, who then helped Santa fill the socks and pillowcases of the sleeping children of New Zealand. They put the big presents carefully on the floor at the ends of their beds.

'Just enough time to visit Australia and then take you home to Lagrangeville,' Santa said to Nicholas.
It was quite warm when they landed.
Without snow the reindeer moved more swiftly across the ground.

'Australia should be easy,' whispered Nicholas. 'Many children put their names on pillowcases pinned to their bed ends.'
Santa moved so quickly in and out of the houses that before Nicholas could blink, he had finished!

Back in the sleigh, Santa peered into his almost empty sack.

'Now, I wonder who these presents are for?' He chuckled as he lifted them out. The Christmas angel sprinkled some stardust on the presents and they disappeared.

'And now,' said Santa, 'let's take you home.'

Nicholas stayed awake for as long as he could. As the dawn light grew in the eastern sky, his eyelids grew heavy. Soon his head fell dreaming onto Santa's elbow - which was soft and warm, just like a pillow...

Santa turned to his little helper and whispered, 'It doesn't really matter how children get their presents or whether they have chimneys in their homes - it's the message of love that comes with each present, that's the important thing.' The sleigh sped through the pale dawn light taking home one special little helper before returning Santa to the North Pole.

On Christmas morning Nicholas awoke:
Was it just a dream?
He ran to the mantelpiece. The glass was empty - and on the plate only a few crumbs remained.
But best of all, next to the Christmas Tree were presents for Peter, Taylor and Peter and... Nicholas. And on each present was a tiny sparkle of stardust!